**To Stan
and Sky**

Author's Note
Readers might be interested to know
that beneath its colorful tail feathers
a peacock has a plain tail that helps
it raise and spread its train.

Book design by Kristen M. Nobles.
Typeset in Ad Lib and BaseNine.
The illustrations in this book were carved in shina plywood
and printed in watercolor paint on Japanese rice paper.

Manufactured in Hong Kong.

Library of Congress Cataloging-in-Publication Data
Araki, Mie.
Perfect tail : a Fred and Lulu story / Mie Araki.
p. cm.
Summary: Fred stops being envious of other animals' tails when his
friendship with Lulu helps him to learn to like himself.
ISBN 0-8118-4266-5
[1. Self-acceptance—Fiction. 2. Tail—Fiction. 3. Rabbits—Fiction.
4. Rhinoceroses—Fiction. 5. Animals—Fiction.] I. Title.
PZ7.A663Pe 2004
[E]—dc22
2003022182

Distributed in Canada by Raincoast Books
9050 Shaughnessy Street, Vancouver, British Columbia V6P 6E5

10 9 8 7 6 5 4 3 2 1

Chronicle Books LLC
85 Second Street, San Francisco, California 94105

www.chroniclekids.com

The Perfect Tail

A Fred and Lulu Story

Mie Araki

chronicle books · san francisco

One day, Fred met Rodney by the stream.
"Lovely day for laundry, isn't it?"
said Rodney.

But Fred didn't answer.

He was too busy admiring Rodney's striped tail.

He thought about it all the way home.

"I wish I had a striped tail like Rodney's," he said.

So he painted a beautiful stripe on his tail—

but it washed away in the shower.

The next day, Fred met Myrtle at the playground.

"Great day for swinging," said Myrtle.
"Care to join me?"

But Fred was speechless with admiration.

He couldn't take his eyes off Myrtle's long tail.

He thought about it all the way home.

"I wish I had a long tail like Myrtle's," he said.

So he tied a long ribbon to his own tail—

but it got all tangled up with his jump rope.

The next day, Fred went for a picnic with Peter.

"Aren't these sunflower seeds delicious?"
said Peter.

But Fred couldn't eat.

He was all choked up over Peter's colorful tail.

He thought about it all the way home.

"I wish I had a colorful tail like Peter's," he said.

So he glued bright feathers all over his tail—

but they fell off when he danced.

The next day, Fred met Penny eating flowers.

"Care for a snack?"
said Penny.

But Fred could only gasp.

Penny's spiky tail took his breath away.

He thought about it all the way home.

"I wish I had a spiky tail like Penny's,"
he said.

So he stuck a bunch of toothpicks onto his tail—

but then he couldn't sit down. Ouch!

The next day, Fred was going swimming
when he heard a voice say,
"What a fine tail you have."

Fred turned around.
"You mean me?" he said.

"Of course," said Lulu.
"It's not too stripy. It's not too long.
It's not too colorful. It's not too spiky. It's perfect.
Want to go swimming?"

So Fred and Lulu went swimming together, and Fred didn't have to worry about his stripe washing off.

**They had a picnic together,
and Fred's tail didn't hurt a bit
when he sat down.**

**They danced together,
and no feathers fell off of Fred's tail.**

They jumped rope together, and Fred's tail didn't get tangled up at all.

"Thank you, Lulu," said Fred.
"This was a wonderful day."

"You're welcome, Fred," said Lulu.
"I had a good time, too."

"And ... er ..." said Fred,
"you have a wonderful horn."

"Thank you," said Lulu.
"I thought you'd never notice."